Spotter's Guide to

SHELLS

An introduction to seashells of the world

Graham D. Saunders
Honorary Secretary of The British Shell Collectors' Club

Special Consultant
Dr W. K. Emerson
Curator of Living and Fossil Invertebrae,
American Museum of Natural History, New York

Photography by Mike Freeman

Illustrated by Andy Martin

Contents

3 What is a shell?
4 How to use this book
6 Gastropods
37 Bivalves
47 Chitons and Tusk Shells
48 Cephalopods
49 Parts of a shell
50 How shells grow
51 Biology of a mollusc
52 Life cycle of a mollusc
53 How a mollusc moves
54 Where shells live
55 Rocky and sandy shores
56 Muddy shores and coral
57 Collecting shells
58 Cleaning and storing shells
59 Books to read
Useful addresses
60 Glossary
61 Checklist
63 Index

Designed by
Cloud Nine Design

Edited by
Helen Gilks and
Lauris Morgan-Griffiths

First published in 1979 by
Usborne Publishing Limited,
Usborne House
83-85 Saffron Hill
London EC1N 8RT, England

Text and Artwork © 1992, 1979 by
Usborne Publishing Limited

Printed in Great Britain

Universal edition

What is a shell?

Shells are the protective covering of soft-bodied animals called molluscs. The name mollusc comes from the Latin *mollis* meaning soft. When the animals that live inside shells die, the shells are left free to drift in the sea. Many of them are washed up on the seashore. This book helps you to identify some of the many thousands of different kinds of sea shells that are found all over the world.

Classes

Over the millions of years molluscs have evolved in different ways. Scientists have divided them into six "classes". Each class has a distinct type of shell. The five major classes are:

1. Gastropoda
(Snails, limpets, whelks, etc.) Gastropods have a single shell which is usually coiled.

2. Bivalvia

(Cockles, mussels, oysters, etc.) Bivalves have two shells (valves) usually unequal in size, and joined by a hinge.

3. Cephalopoda
(Squid, octopus, cuttle-fish). Some cephalopods have no shell; in others the shell is outside the animal, or inside the animal's soft body. They all have tentacles.

5. Scaphopoda

4. Amphineura
(Chitons) have a flexible shell made up of eight overlapping plates.

(Tusk shells). Scaphopods begin life as tiny bivalves. The two valves fuse together to form a tapering tube which is open at both ends.

This book shows examples of the first five of the six classes. When you find a shell, first decide which of these classes it belongs to and turn to that section in the book. Leaf through until you see a shell similar to the one you have found.

In each section of the book you will find several individual species, or kinds, of shells. We cannot show all the different species of shells that exist in the world (there are about 100,000), so we have shown only a selection.

3

How to use this book

What is a species?

All the species in this book are molluscs, but they are organized, or classified, into smaller groups to show their similarities.

Molluscs are divided first into classes, then families, genera (singular "genus") and finally into species. Classification does not only depend on the similarity in appearance of the shells, but on the biology and behaviour of the animal.

Each individual shell is a separate **species.** Shells of the same species breed together and nearly always look the same. A group of species which look similar but do not breed together is called a **genus.** A group of genera that have similar characteristics but do not necessarily look alike is called a **family.**

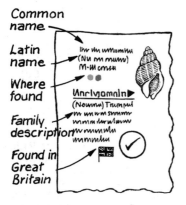

Common name

Latin name

Where found

Family description

Found in Great Britain

Why use Latin names?

Latin names are used because in many cases there is no common name for a shell. Common names change; the Latin name never does.

The Latin name of a species is made up of two words. The first word is the genus name, and starts with a capital letter. The second is the name of the particular species and starts with a small letter.

What's on a page.

On each page is a description of a family. When you find a shell that looks like the one you want to identify, read the description to check that your shell belongs to that family. The description tells you the common name and the Latin name, where those shells are found, and a general description of their colour and shape.

See page 49 for a labelled drawing showing the different features of a shell.

Beside each family description there is a blank circle. If your shell belongs to that family, tick it off.

At the back of the book is a checklist to record the date and place where you found your shells. Below each family description is a symbol. This shows which shell families can be found in Britain (flag) or North America (map). You may find some families in a shell shop or museum.

In addition to the family description, there is a small caption next to each species illustrated. This gives its common and Latin name, maximum size and a coloured circle to show where in the world it can be found (see page 5).

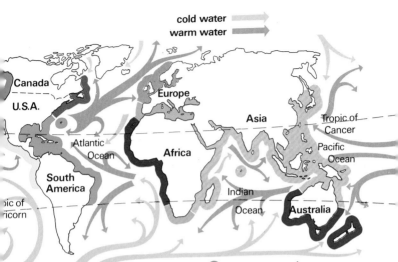

cold water
warm water

Canada
U.S.A.
Europe
Asia
Tropic of Cancer
Atlantic Ocean
Africa
Pacific Ocean
South America
Indian Ocean
Australia
Tropic of Capricorn

The description for each family of shells tells you what type of water that family prefers: tropical, warm or cold. Tropical means in the area between the two tropics (see above). The warm and cold regions of the seas are marked on the map.

Different species that are members of the same family of shells will generally be found living in similar conditions – cold or warm water – although one species may live in one part of the world, and another thousands of miles away.

You can find out where the species illustrated in this book live by looking at the small coloured circles after the name of the species. These colours refer to the areas of the world shown on the map.

Indo-Pacific. Warm to tropical waters. A large number of colourful and attractive species. Probably the richest area in the world for shells.

Australia and New Zealand. Many different families and species; many of them colourful.

Northwest America. Cool waters. Shells tend to be hardy and strong. A few are colourful.

Panamic. Warm waters. Rich in colourful shells. Fewer species than in Indo-Pacific.

Caribbean. Warm waters. Many different species. Some of the largest species of shells are from this area.

Northeast America. Temperate to cold waters. Shells tend to be strong and heavy. Large numbers are white or brown.

Northwest Europe. Cool waters, in places warm because of Gulf Stream. Few colourful shells.

Mediterranean. Warm waters. A few colourful shells, generally rather small.

West Africa. Sub-tropical to tropical waters. Shells of this area are fast-growing and many are colourful.

South Africa. Cool waters. Strong shells, several colourful species.

5

Keyhole

Keyhole Limpets

(Fissurellidae). Tropical and warm seas. Cap-shaped shells; most species have a small keyhole shape in the top. On rocks, near low water line.

▲
Green Panama Keyhole
(Fissurella virescens)
● 4cm (1½").

Roman Shield ▶
(Scutus antipodes)
10cm (4"). Australia
●●

◀
Italian Keyhole
(Diodora italica)
5cm (2"). ●

Limpets

(Patellidae). Warm and tropical seas. Flattened cone-shaped shells, evenly shaped. More pointed shells come from rough waters. Several hundred species.

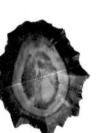

Eye Limpet
(Patella oculus)
10cm (4").●

Tortoiseshell Limpet ▼
(Acmea testudinalis)
2.5cm (1"). ●●

▲ **Mediterranean Limpet**
(Patella caerulea)
●● 6cm (2⅓").

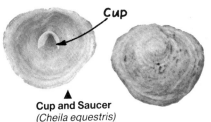

Cup and Saucer
(Cheila equestris)
2.5cm (1").

Hoof Shells

(Hipponicidae) Worldwide. Cap-shaped, non-spiral shells. Found in shallow waters. White shells usually stained yellow or brown. Often attached to other shells.

◄ Horse's Hoof
(Amalthea antiquata)
2cm (¾").

Slipper Limpets/Crucibles

(Calyptraeidae) Worldwide. Flattened shells, often non-spiral. Thin shelf inside the shell. Often attached to other shells or stones. Smooth and evenly shaped.

Hungarian Cap
(Capulus ungaricus)
5cm (2").

Slipper Limpet ▼
(Crepidula fornicata)
5cm (2").

Shelf

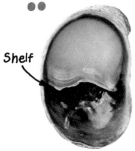

▲ Peruvian Hat
(Trochatella trochiformis)
7cm (2¾").

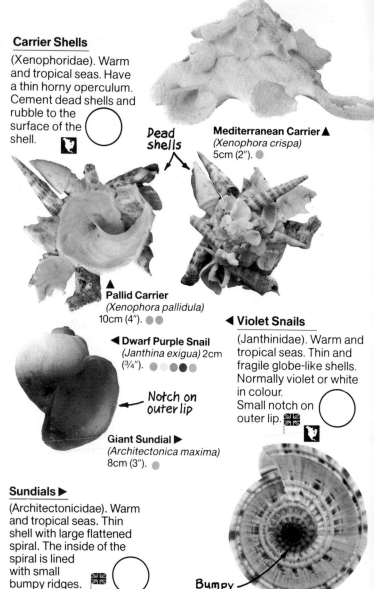

Carrier Shells

(Xenophoridae). Warm and tropical seas. Have a thin horny operculum. Cement dead shells and rubble to the surface of the shell.

Dead shells

Mediterranean Carrier ▲
(Xenophora crispa)
5cm (2"). ●

▲
Pallid Carrier
(Xenophora pallidula)
10cm (4"). ●●

◀ **Dwarf Purple Snail**
(Janthina exigua) 2cm
(¾"). ● ● ● ● ●

Notch on outer lip

Giant Sundial ▶
(Architectonica maxima)
8cm (3"). ●

◀ **Violet Snails**

(Janthinidae). Warm and tropical seas. Thin and fragile globe-like shells. Normally violet or white in colour.
Small notch on outer lip.

Sundials ▶

(Architectonicidae). Warm and tropical seas. Thin shell with large flattened spiral. The inside of the spiral is lined with small bumpy ridges.

Bumpy ridge

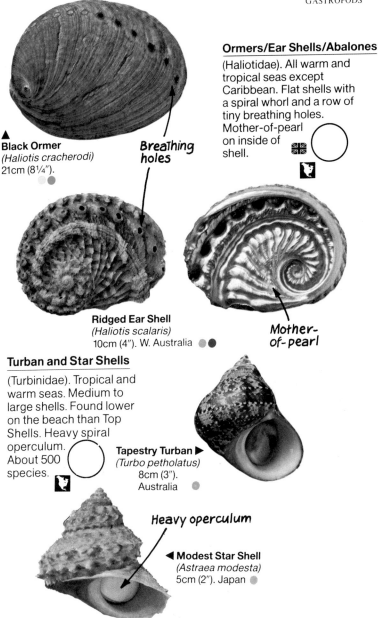

▲ **Black Ormer**
(Haliotis cracherodi)
21cm (8¼").

Breathing holes

Ormers/Ear Shells/Abalones

(Haliotidae). All warm and tropical seas except Caribbean. Flat shells with a spiral whorl and a row of tiny breathing holes. Mother-of-pearl on inside of shell.

Ridged Ear Shell
(Haliotis scalaris)
10cm (4"). W. Australia ●●

Mother-of-pearl

Turban and Star Shells

(Turbinidae). Tropical and warm seas. Medium to large shells. Found lower on the beach than Top Shells. Heavy spiral operculum. About 500 species.

Tapestry Turban ▶
(Turbo petholatus)
8cm (3").
Australia ●

Heavy operculum

◀ **Modest Star Shell**
(Astraea modesta)
5cm (2"). Japan ●

9

Top Shells (p. 10-11)

(Trochidae). Worldwide. Shells from deep water are pointed and thin with fine surface sculpture; shells from shallow water are heavy and rounded. Round, horny operculum. Inside the shell is mother-of-pearl.

Pyramid Top Shell ▲
(Tectus pyramis) 10cm (4").

▲ Yellow Sponge Top Shell
(Calliostoma monile)
2.5cm (1").
N. Australia

Radiant Top Shell ▼
(Trochus radiatus)
4cm (1½").
Indian Ocean

◄ Kelp Top Shell
(Calliostoma bonita)
3cm (1¼").

Snake Skin Top Shell ►
(Tegula pellisserpentis)
3cm (1¼").

◀ Coral Top
(Gibbula corallinoides)
2.5cm (1"). ●

Lined Top ▶
(Monodonta lineata)
3cm (1¼"). ●

Mother-of-pearl ──

Strawberry Top ▶
(Clanculus pharonium)
2.5cm (1").
Indian Ocean ●

▲ Pheasant Shell
(Phasianella ventricosa)
3cm (1¼").
●

● **Dolphin Shell ▶**
(Angaria delphinula)
8cm (3").

11

Periwinkles/Winkles

(Littorinidae). Worldwide. Cold-water shells are rounded and heavy. Tropical shells are thinner and high-spired.

Flat Periwinkle ▶
(Littorina littoralis)
1.5cm (½").
● ●

▲
Southern Periwinkle
(Littorina angulifera)
● 3cm (1¼").

▲
Chameleon Nerite
(Nerita chameleon)
3cm (1¼"). Australia ●

Nerite Snails

(Neritidae). Tropical and warm seas. Strong and often colourful. Broad body whorl. Hook on operculum.

Hook on operculum

◀ **Bleeding Tooth**
(Nerita peloronta)
● 4cm (1½").

Turrets/Screw Shells ▶

(Turritellidae). Warm and tropical seas. Long thin spiral shells live buried in sand or mud below low water line.

◀ **European Screw Shell**
(Turritella communis)
4cm (1½").
● ●

Round opening

Common Cerith
(Cerithum vulgatum)
● 8cm (3″).

◄ Horn Shells/Needle Whelks

(Cerithidae). Worldwide, but more common in tropical seas. Identified by siphonal canal which twists back. Moves about on weed or rock.

Banded Creeper ►
(Rhinoclavis fasciatus)
8cm (3″). ●

Siphonal canal

Ribs

Precious Wentletrap ►
(Epitonium scalare)
7.5cm (3″). ●

Wentletraps ►

(Epitoniidae). Worldwide. Round opening. Colour white, grey or brown with thin, round, dark-coloured operculum. Notice ribs on shell.

◄ Crenulated Wentletrap
(Opalia crenata)
3cm (1¼″).
● ● ●

Lance Auger ►
(Terebra lanceata)
8cm (3″).
W. Pacific ●

◄ Augers

(Terebridae). Tropical and warm seas. Long, thin spire. Augers distinguished from Turret and Horn shells by shape of siphonal canal.

Siphonal canal →

Knorr's Worm
(Vermicularia knorri)
● 10cm (4").

◀ Worm Shells
(Vermetidae). Warm and tropical seas. Young shells shaped like pointed turrets, but then grow unevenly into "worm-like" shapes.
About 50 species.

Turrids ▶
(Turridae). Worldwide. Small shells with notch at the suture. Small opening. Horny operculum. More than 1,200 species. Up to 15cm (6").

◀ Rose Turrid
(Clavus rosalina)
● 4cm (1½").

— *Notch*

Tun Shells
(Tonnidae). Tropical and warm seas. Large thin shells with spiral ridges. Colour white, yellow or brown. Often damaged when found on beaches.

◀ Partridge Tun
(Tonna perdix)
20cm (8"). ●

Banded Tun ▼
(Tonna sulcosa) 12cm (5").
●

◀ Fig Shells

(Ficidae). Tropical seas, except W. Africa. Long siphonal canal. Finely sculptured with criss-crossed surface. Less than 15 species.

◀ Spotted Fig
(Ficus ficoides)
● 10cm (4").

Moon Snails/Necklace Shells

(Naticidae). Worldwide. Strong, shiny shells which can be thick, rounded or flattened. Small spire with few whorls. Large opening. Operculum is usually semicircular.

Shark Eye ▲
(Polinices duplicatus)
●● 8cm (3").

◀ Baby Ear
(Sinum perspectivum) 4cm (1½").
●●

Colourful Atlantic Moon Snail ▶
(Naticarius canrena)
●● 4cm (1½").

◀ Lightning Moon Shell
(Natica fulminea)
● 3cm (1¼").

◀ **Hunter's Tulip**
(Fasciolaria hunteria)
10cm (4″).

Tulip Shells

(Fasciolariidae). Tropical
and warm seas. Smooth
columella with fine tooth-
like marks on outer lip.
Living animal is usually
bright red. Smooth shell
with thick, hairy
or smooth, thin
periostracum.

Distaff Spindle ▶
(Fusinus colus)
20cm (8″).

Columella

Fischer's Tulip ▶
(Fasciolaria buxea)
10cm (4″).

◀ **Needle Tooth**
*(Opeatostoma
pseudodon)*
4.5cm (1¾″).

Knobbly Latirus ▲
(Latirus polygonus)
8cm (3″).

◄ Atlantic Triton
(Charonia variegata)
40cm (16"). ●●●

Varix

Angular Triton ▶
(Cymatium femorale)
18cm (7"). ●

Hairy Tritons
(Cymatidae). Tropical and warm seas. Usually covered with hairy periostracum. Pointed siphonal canal. One or more varices. About 100 species.

Distorsio Triton
(Distortio reticulata)
6cm (2⅓").

Nutmegs ▶
(Cancellariidae). Warm and tropical seas. Three or more heavy folds on columella. Sculpture on shell gives latticed effect. Oval-shaped operculum.

◄ Common Nutmeg
(Cancellaria reticulata)
4cm (1½"). ●

Folds

Varices

Blood Stained ▶ Frog Shell
(Bursa cruentata)
4cm (1½").
●●●●

Canals

◄ Frog Shells
(Bursidae). Tropical and warm seas. Two distinct canals from the opening. One or more varices which may form "wings" at the side of the shell.

17

Murex Shells (p.18-19)

(Muricidae). Worldwide, but most are tropical. Long or short siphonal canal. Shells have spines, knobs or horns like wings. Operculum dark brown and horny. Some live on rocks, but more delicate shells are found on mud. Several hundred species.

Venus Comb ▶
(Murex pecten)
● 15cm (6").

Dye Murex ▶
(Bolinus brandaris)
10cm (4"). ●●

Stainforth's Murex ▲
(Hexaplex stainforthi)
6.5cm (2½").
N.W. Australia ●

Callidan ▶
(Muricanthus callidinus)
10cm (4").
●

◀ Ramose Murex
(Chicoreus ramosus)
● 30cm (12").

◄ **Leafy Horn Mouth**
(Ceratostoma foliatus)
10cm (4"). ●

Three Winged Rock Shell ▶
(Pteropurpura trialata)
● ● 8.5cm (3⅓").

◄ **Murex Pinnatus**
(Pterynotus alatus)
7cm (2¾").
S.E. Asia ●

▲
Cuming's Typhis
(Typhis cumingi)
2.5cm (1"). ●

Zambo's Murex
(Homalocantha zamboi)
6cm (2⅓").
Philippines ● ▶

Rock Shells/Dye Shells

(Thaididae). Worldwide. Solid, low-spired shells with a large body whorl. Wide opening. Operculum red/brown, thin and horny. Usually small knobs around the shell. On rocks between high and low water.

◀ **Garland Thaid**
(Nassa serta)
7cm (2¾").
E. Australia ●

Rock Shell ▶
(Thais haemastoma)
●●● 8cm (3").

◀ **Red Mouth Drupe**
(Drupa rubusidaea)
5.5cm
(2¼"). ●

Wide Mouth Rock Shell ▶
(Purpura patula) 10cm
(4"). ●

◀ **Cart Rut Shell**
(Neothais scalaris)
10cm (4").
New Zealand ●

◀ **Violet Coral Snail**
(Coralliophila neritoidea)
6cm (2⅓″).

Coral Snails

(Coralliophilidae). Warm
and tropical seas. Round,
often spiny, with many
small spiral ridges.
Mostly white
and often live
near coral.

◀ **Meyendorff's Coral Snail**
(Coralliophila meyendorffi)
4cm (1½″).

◀ **Mawa's Pagoda**
(Latiaxis mawae) 7cm (2¾″).
Japan

False Triton ▶
(Colubraria reticulata)
3.5cm (1⅓″).

False Tritons

(Colubrariidae). Tropical
seas. Different from real
Tritons by thickening of
the shell near the opening.
Under rocks
in shallow
water.

*Thickening
of shell*

Giant False Triton ▶
(Colubraria maculosa)
10cm (4″). W. Pacific

21

Unicolour Dog Whelk ▼
(Zeuxis dorsatus) 3cm
(1¼"). W. Australia ●

Thickened lip

Moroccan Bullia ▶
(Bullia miran)
3.5cm (1⅓"). ●

Dog Whelks

(Nassariidae). Worldwide.
Most have latticed
sculpture. Short siphonal
canal is slightly twisted.
Lip is thicker than
the rest of the
shell. 🇬🇧

Whelk ▶
(Buccinum undatum)
15cm ●●
(6").

Siphonal canal →

Wolff's Dog Whelk ▲
(Nassarius wolffi)
5cm (2"). ●

Whelks

(Buccinidae). Worldwide.
Similar to Dog Whelks, but
usually larger and in
mature shells the lip is
thinner than
the rest of the
shell. Thick
periostracum.

Channeled Babylon ▶
(Babylonia canaliculata)
7cm. (2¾").
N. Indian Ocean ●

◀
**New England
Neptune**
*(Neptunea
decemcostata)*
● 12cm (5").

No thickening of lip

Helmet Shells

(Cassidae). Tropical seas.
Large, heavy shells often
with wide strong lips.
Teeth on one or both lips.
Siphonal canal twists and
turns back.
About 80
species.

King Helmet ▲
(Cassis tuberosa)
23cm (9"). ● ●

canal
twists back

Bull Mouth ▶
(Cypraecassis rufa)
● 18cm (7").

◀ Scotch Bonnet
(Phalium granulatum) 7cm
(2¾") ● ● ●

Lip
teeth

Japanese Bonnet ▶
(Phalium bisulcatum)
● 7cm (2¾").

23

Spider Stromb ▶
(Lambis lambis)
20cm (8"). ●

Strombs/Conches (p.24-25)

(Strombidae). Tropical and
warm seas. Young shells
can be mistaken for Cone
Shells before they have
developed their strong,
broad, outer lip. Have
notch at the side, known as
"stromboid notch". Living
animal has brightly
coloured eyes on
long stalks.

Fighting Conch ▶
(Strombus pugilus).
● 9cm (3½").

*Stromboid
notch*

Scorpion Stromb ▶
(Lambis scorpius)
● 15cm (6").

◀ Lister's Conch
(Strombus listeri)
15cm (6").
S.E. Asia ●

Spindle Tibia ▶
(Tibia fusus)
20cm. (8").
Philippines

Sail Strombus ▶
(Strombus epidromus)
9cm (3½").
Pacific

◀
Granular Stromb
(Strombus granulatus)
8cm (3").

Powis' Tibia ▶
(Tibia powisi)
5cm (2").
Pacific

▶
Martin's Tibia
(Tibia martini)
15cm (6").
Philippines

◀ Dwarf Tibia
(Varicospira cancellata)
3cm (1¼").
Pacific

◀ **Ostrich Foot**
(Struthiolaria papulosa)
9cm (3½").
New Zealand ●

↙ Thickened lip

Ostrich Foot Shells ▶

(Struthiolaridae). New Zealand, Australia and Indian Ocean. Fragile, brown shells with thickened lip. Heavy white thickening by opening.

West African Bird Foot ▶
(Aporrhais senegalensis)
3cm (1¼").
●

Pelican Foot/Duck Foot Shells

(Aporrhaidae). N. Atlantic, Mediterranean, W. Africa. Wide lip, usually with straight spines. Only 5 to 6 living species.

Pelican's Foot
◀ *(Aporrhais pespelicani)*
6cm (2⅓").
● ●

Snipe Head ▶
(Tudicula inermis)
8cm (3").
N.W. Australia ●

Vase Shells

(Vasidae). Tropical seas. Heavy shells, usually white with dark markings on their blunt spines. Has a hairy periostracum.

Vase Shell ▶
(Vasum muricatum)
13cm (5¼").
●

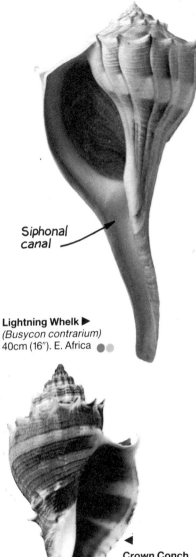

Crown Conches

(Melongenidae). Tropical seas. Short-spired heavy shell with long siphonal canal. Periostracum is usually thick and rather rubbery. Feeds on other molluscs.

Siphonal canal

Lightning Whelk ▶
(Busycon contrarium)
40cm (16"). E. Africa ●●

Crown Conch
(Melongena corona)
10cm (4"). ●

Fig Whelk
(Busycon spiratum)
13cm (5¼"). ●●

27

◀ Rose Harp
(Harpa doris)
7.5cm (3"). ●

Varices

Harp Shells

(Harpidae). Tropical seas.
Attractive shells with
obvious varices which
show growth
stages.
About
12 species.

Articulated Harp ▶
(Harpa articularis)
10cm (4").
W. Pacific ●

Cone Shells

(Conidae). Tropical seas.
Uniform cone or
cylinder-type shells with
long, narrow opening.
Some have
poisonous
sting.

Court Cone ▶
(Conus aulicus)
● 7cm (2¾").

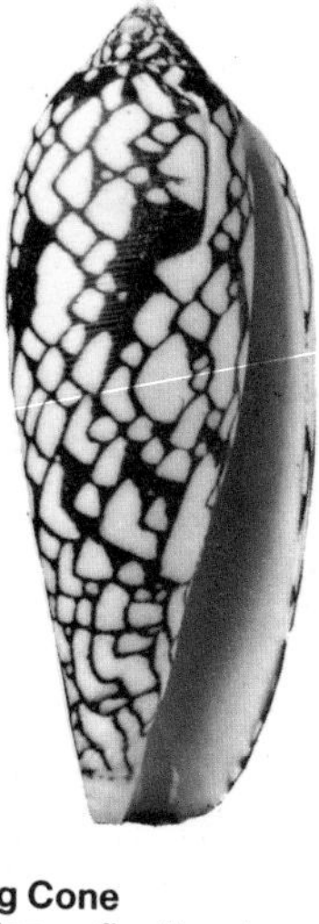

◀ Fig Cone
(Conus figulinus)
● 8cm (3").

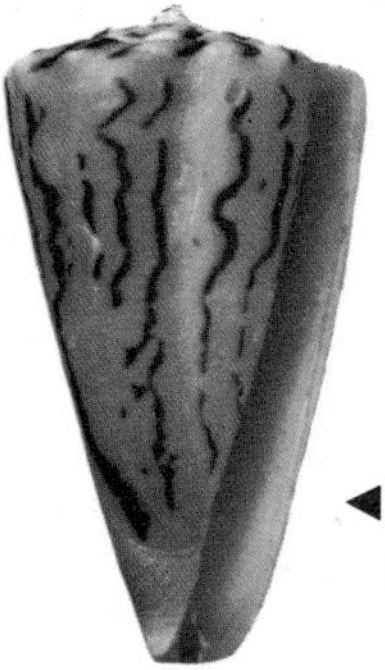

◀ Prince Cone
(Conus princep
7cm (2¾").

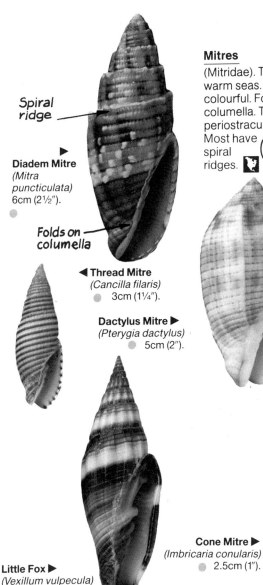

Spiral ridge

► **Diadem Mitre**
(Mitra puncticulata)
6cm (2½").

Folds on columella

Mitres

(Mitridae). Tropical and warm seas. Slim, long and colourful. Folds on columella. Thin periostracum. Most have spiral ridges.

◄ **Thread Mitre**
(Cancilla filaris)
3cm (1¼").

Dactylus Mitre ►
(Pterygia dactylus)
5cm (2").

Cone Mitre ►
(Imbricaria conularis)
2.5cm (1").

Little Fox ►
(Vexillum vulpecula)
7cm (2¾").
W. Pacific

Margin Shells

(Marginellidae). Warm and
tropical seas. Spire short
or covered by body whorl.
Usually 3-5 folds on
columella. Thick outer lip.
No periostracum.
Smooth, shiny
shells.

Thick
outer
lip

Folds on
columella

◀ **Desjardin's Margin**
(Marginella desjardini)
7cm (2¾").

◀
Orange Margin
(Prunum oblonga)
2.5cm (1").

Striper Margin ▶
(Persicula cingula)
2cm (¾").

◀ **Loup Margin**
(Persicula phyrgia)
0.5cm (1¼").

Philippine Margin ▶
(Volvarina philippinarium)
1.5cm (⅔").
W. Pacific

▲ **Pink Margin**
(Marginella irrorata)
3cm (1¼").

30

Olives

(Olividae). Tropical and warm seas. Smooth, shiny shells. Short spire. Body whorl is almost whole length of shell. Long opening with small folds on inner lip.

Tent Olive ▶
(Oliva porphyria)
15cm (6″).

Folds on inner lip →

◀ Red Mouth Olive
(Oliva mineacea)
10cm (4″).

Fat Olive ▶
(Olivancillaria gibbosa)
5cm (2″).

◀ Lady Olive
(Olivella dama)
2.5cm (1″).

◀ Long Ancilla
(Amalda elongata)
5cm (2″).
N. Australia

Hebrew Volute ▶
(Voluta ebraea)
● 15cm (6″).

Volutes (p. 32-33)
(Volutidae). Temperate,
warm and tropical seas;
especially in Australia.
Shells mostly thick, shiny,
heavy and colourful.
Usually large protoconch,
which is often
smooth and
rounded.

◀
Cuming's Volute
(Lyria cumingi)
3.5cm (1⅓″).

◀
Algarve Volute
(Cymbium olla)
13cm (5¼″).
●

Imperial Volute ▶
(Cymbiola imperialis)
25cm (10″).
Philppines

Smooth protoconch

◀ Baler Shell
(Melo amphorus)
25cm (10″).
W. Pacific
●

32

◄ Neptune Volute
(Neptuniopsis gilchristi)
20cm (8"). ●

Hallia ►
(Ampulla priamus)
9cm (3½").
Spain and Portugal ●

◄ Damon's Volute
(Amoria damoni)
15cm (6").
Australia ●

◄ Junonia Volute
(Scaphella junonia)
14cm (5¾"). ●

Beautiful Volute ►
(Cymbiolaca pulchra)
9cm (3½").
N. E. Australia ●

◄ Snowflake Volute
(Aulicina nivosa)
8.5cm (3⅓").
W. Australia ●

*Two varieties of
Snowflake Volute*

Humpback Cowrie
(Cypraea decipiens)
6cm (2⅓"). W. Australia
▼

▲ **Sieve Cowrie**
(Cypraea cribraria)
3.5cm (1⅓"). ●

Teeth on both lips

◀ **Atlantic Cowrie**
(Cypraea spurca)
●●● 3cm (1¼").

◀ **Little Deer Cowrie**
(Cypraea cervinetta) 9cm
(3½"). ●

Cowries

(Cypraeidae). Tropical and
warm seas. Body whorl
forms the whole shell.
Shiny, smooth shells with
a row of "teeth" on
both lips.
About 180
species.

European Cowrie
(Trivia monacha)
◀ 1.5cm (⅔").
●●●

Button Shells

(Eratoidae). Tropical and
warm seas. Small shells
similar to Cowries but with
grooves across the back
of shell.
Many are
microshells.

Grooves

Radiant Button Shell ▶
(Trivia radians)
● 2cm (¾").

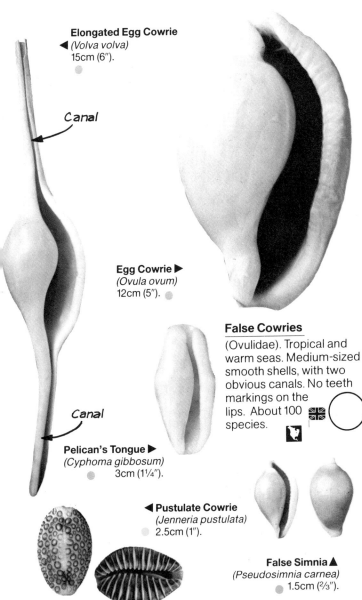

Elongated Egg Cowrie
◄ *(Volva volva)*
15cm (6″).

Canal

Egg Cowrie ►
(Ovula ovum)
12cm (5″).

Canal

Pelican's Tongue ►
(Cyphoma gibbosum)
3cm (1¼″).

◄ **Pustulate Cowrie**
(Jenneria pustulata)
2.5cm (1″).

False Cowries

(Ovulidae). Tropical and warm seas. Medium-sized smooth shells, with two obvious canals. No teeth markings on the lips. About 100 species.

False Simnia ▲
(Pseudosimnia carnea)
1.5cm (⅔″).

◀ **Rustic Dove Shell**
(Pyrene rustica)
2.5cm (1"). ● ●

Dove Shells

(Pyrenidae). Warm and
tropical seas. Strong, small,
colourful shells. Often in
large numbers in seaweed.
Usually covered
in lime or weed
when alive.

(Strombina dorsata) ▶
● 3cm (1¼"):

Bubble Shells

(Opisthobrachia). Tropical
and warm seas. Thin,
fragile shells. Thin outer lip.
Sunken spire.
Found in
sand and mud.

*Sunken
spire*

**White
Banded
Bubble** ▶
*(Hydatina
albocincta)*
6cm (2⅓").
●

Canoe Shell ▶
(Scaphander lignarius)
● ● 7cm (2¾").

◀ **Pacific Bubble**
(Bulla ampulla)
● 6cm (2⅓").

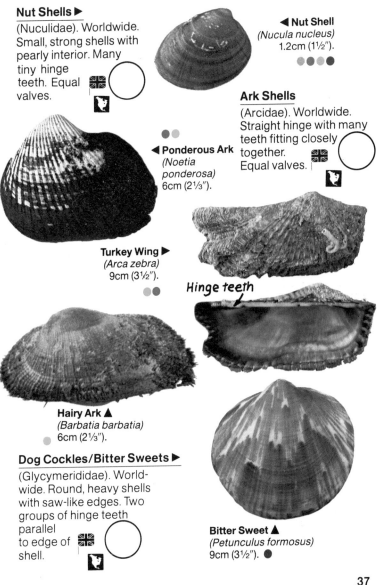

Nut Shells ▶

(Nuculidae). Worldwide. Small, strong shells with pearly interior. Many tiny hinge teeth. Equal valves.

◀ **Nut Shell**
(Nucula nucleus)
1.2cm (1½").

◀ **Ponderous Ark**
(Noetia ponderosa)
6cm (2⅓").

Ark Shells

(Arcidae). Worldwide. Straight hinge with many teeth fitting closely together. Equal valves.

Turkey Wing ▶
(Arca zebra)
9cm (3½").

Hinge teeth

Hairy Ark ▲
(Barbatia barbatia)
6cm (2⅓").

Dog Cockles/Bitter Sweets ▶

(Glycymerididae). World-wide. Round, heavy shells with saw-like edges. Two groups of hinge teeth parallel to edge of shell.

Bitter Sweet ▲
(Petunculus formosus)
9cm (3½"). ●

Horse Mussel ▶
(Modiolus modiolus)
22cm (8½″).
●●

Blue Mussel ▲
(Mytilus edulis)
●● 12cm (5″).

◀ Date Mussel
(Lithophaga lithophaga)
● 7cm (2¾″).

Mussels

(Mytilidae). Worldwide.
Blue or brown. Live
attached to rocks by
threads. Valves are equal
size and do not
have teeth.
Edible.
Very common.

Yellow Mussel
◀ *(Brachidontes citrinus)*
5cm (2″). ●

▼ Radiant Cardita
(Cardita radians)
4.5cm (1¾″). ●

European Cardita ▶
(Cardita calyculata)
●● 2.5cm (1″).

◀ Carditas

(Carditidae). Worldwide.
Small, often elongated,
shells with distinct ribs.
Equal valves. One major
hinge tooth. Under
stones in
shallow water.

Saw-like edge

Cockles

(Cardidae). Worldwide. Heart-shaped shell. Most have strong ribs with saw-like edges. Two central teeth on hinge, and usually one or two teeth on each side of the hinge.

◀ China Cockle
(Trachycardium egmontianum)
4cm (1½″).

Egg Cockle ▶
(Laevicardium laevigatum)
4cm (1½″).

◀ Long Giant Clam
(Tridacna elongata)
32cm (12½″).

Giant Clams

(Tridacnidae). Tropical areas of Indo-Pacific. Large, thick, heavy shells. Gap near the hinge through which the mollusc anchors itself. Six species.

Gap

Fluted Giant Clam ▼
(Tridacna squamosa)
40cm (16″).

Flat Oyster ▲
(Isognomon isognomon)
●●●○● 12cm (5").

◀Hammer Oysters

(Isognominidae). Tropical parts of Atlantic and Pacific. Flat shells with a long, straight row of hinge teeth.

Hinge teeth

Blue pearly interior

◀ Hammer Oysters

(Malleidae). Tropical Indo-Pacific. Wide base and narrow body. Blue pearly interior near the hinge.

White Hammer Oyster ▶
(Malleus albus)
● 20cm (8").

Pearl Oyster ▶
(Pinctada margaritifera)
18cm (7"). ●

Pearl Oysters

(Pteriidae). Tropical and warm seas. Outside is scaly, inside is mother-of-pearl. Wing-like extensions on hinge.

Mother-of-pearl

Hole

Saddle Oyster ▲
(Anomia ephippium)
⬤⬤⬤ 7cm (2¾").

◄ **Saddle Oysters**
(Anomidae). Worldwide.
Hole in lower valve
through which mollusc
attaches
itself
to rocks.

Two shells
joined
together

Oysters
(Ostreidae). Worldwide.
Large, heavy shells, outer
edges flaky and fragile.
One valve
smaller than
the other.

Cock's Comb ►
(Lopha cristigalli)
⬤ 9cm (3½").

European
oyster
attached
to whelk
shell

European Oyster
(Ostrea edulis)
12cm (5"). ⬤⬤

Beak → ← "Ear"

File Shells ▶

(Limidae). Worldwide. White shells with distinct ribs. Has small "ears" and a beak which extends past the hinge.

◀ **Iredale's Giant File** (*Lima persquamifer*) 10cm (4").

Eastern Lion's Paw ▶ (*Lyropecten corallinoides*) ● 6cm (2⅓").

Scallops

(Pectinidae). Tropical and warm seas. Often colourful. Has an "ear" on either side of beak – one usually larger than the other. Several hundred species.

Pilgrim's Scallop ▶ *"Ear"* (*Pecten jacobaeus*) 15cm (6").

Beak "Ear"

Australian Scallop (*Chlamys austalis*) 9cm (3½"). ▼ Australia ●●

Callico Scallop ▶ (*Aequipecten gibbus*) ●● 50cm (20").

◀ Thorny Oysters

(Spondylidae). Tropical and warm seas. Attaches itself to solid objects. Often has long or short spines.

Oyster attached to coral

◀ Red Thorny Oyster
(Spondylus coccineus)
8cm (3"). ●
Philippines

Jewel Boxes ▶

(Chamidae). Tropical seas. Beak usually strongly curved. Shape varies. Usually covered in seaweed or dead coral.

Leaf Chama
(Chama lazarus) ▶
15cm (6"). ●

Venus Clams

(Veneriidae). Worldwide. Strong, heavy shells. Small but long hinge teeth. Muscle scars on inside of shell.

Kellet's Venus
◀ *(Chione kelletia)*
● 4cm (1½").

Tent Venus ▶
(Lioconcha castrensis)
● 4.5cm (1¾").

Lamellate Venus ▶
(Antigonia lamellaris)
4.5cm (1¾").
W. Pacific ●

43

◀ **Panama Coquina**
(Donax panamensis)
4cm (1½").

Wedge Shells

(Donacidae). Worldwide. Small, shiny, wedge-shaped shell with saw-like edge. Both valves same size.

◀
Great False Coquina
(Iphigenia brasiliensis)
7cm (2¾").

Tellins

(Tellinidae). Worldwide. Flat, thin, usually delicate shell. Stripes of colour on shell. Valves often unequal.

Twist at top

Sunrise Shell ▲
(Tellina radiata) 6cm (2⅓").

Flat Tellin
(Tellina planata)
▼6cm (2⅓").

Sunset Shells ▶

(Psammobiidae). World-
wide. Thin, flat shells.
Similar to Tellins, but more
symmetrical. Equal valves
which have a gap
at each end
when closed.

Stanger's Sanguin ▲
(Gari stangeri)
6cm (2⅓").
New Zealand ●

Trough Shells

(Mactridae). Worldwide.
Heavy and white or fragile
and thin shells. Pale blue
or yellow.
Triangular dent
in hinge.

Violet Surf Clam ▲
(Mactra violacea)
● 8cm (3").

◀ Australian Surf Clam
(Mactra australis)
5cm (2").
N. Australia ●

Beak

Lucines

(Lucinidae). Worldwide.
Thin, round shells. Most
are white. Small
but distinct
beak.

Beak

Orb Lucine ▲
(Codakia orbicularis)
● 8cm (3").

▶
Buttercup Lucine
(Anodonta alba)
●● 5cm (2")

45

◀ **Fan Mussel**
(Pinna rudis)
45cm (18").
●

◀**Fan Mussels/Pen Shells**

(Pinnidae). Tropical and
warm seas. Large, fan-
shaped shell.
No teeth
on hinge.

Piddocks/Angel's Wings▶

(Pholadidae). Worldwide.
Fragile, white shell with
a small spike under the
beak inside
the shell.
No hinge.

Piddock ▲
(Pholas dactylus)
20cm (8").
● ●

Hinge

Razor Shell ▲
(Ensis arcuatus)
17cm (7"). ● ●

◀**Razor Shells**

(Solenidae). Worldwide.
Long, oblong shells. Valves
do not close at either end.
Small hinge at
corner of one
end only.

Chitons

(Amphineura). Worldwide. All species of this class have a shell made up of eight overlapping plates with a leathery girdle. Shell is flexible and smooth or spiny. Difficult to preserve.

▼ **Lined Chiton**
(Tonicella lineata)
4cm (1½").

Leathery girdle

▲ **Spiny Chiton**
(Acanthopleura spinosa)
15cm (6"). N. Australia

◀ **Elephant Tooth**
(Dentalium elephantium)
9cm (3½").

Tusk Shells

(Scaphopoda). Worldwide. Long shells open at both ends. Buried in mud in deep water. Often washed up on beaches after storms. Over 300 species.

◀ **Rosy Tooth**
(Dentalium rubescens)
35cm (14").

47

Brown Paper Nautilus ▶
(Argonauta hians)
75cm (30″).
Worldwide

Paper Nautilus
(Argonauta argo)
◀ 20cm (8″).

Cephalopods

(Cephalapoda). Worldwide.
This class includes squid,
octopus, cuttlefish, and
nautilus. More than
50 species, but only a few
have shells. Almost all have
tentacles, often
with rows of
suckers.

Cuttlefish ▶
(Sepia officinalis)
25cm (10″).
Worldwide

*Horny
transparent
edges*

Ramshorn ▲
(Spirula spirula)
3.5cm (1⅓″).
Worldwide

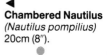

◀
Chambered Nautilus
(Nautilus pompilius)
20cm (8″).

Parts of a shell

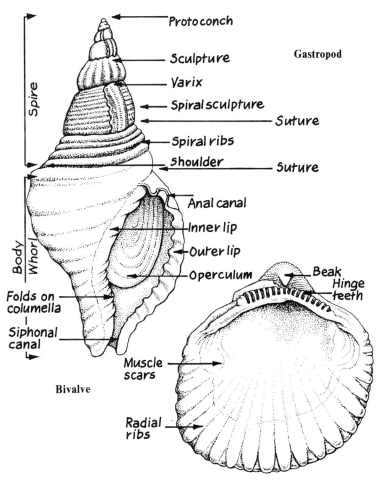

Protoconch

Sculpture

Gastropod

Varix

Spiral sculpture

Suture

Spiral ribs

shoulder

Suture

Anal canal

Inner lip

Outer lip

Operculum

Beak

Hinge teeth

Folds on columella

Siphonal canal

Muscle scars

Bivalve

Radial ribs

Spire

Body Whorl

In the field guide part of the book there is a description of each shell family. A number of species make up a family, so any features in common have been described to help you identify the family.

Above are drawings of a gastro-pod and a bivalve showing their different features and the special words used to name them.

If there are any words you don't understand or if you need further explanation, turn to the Glossary on page 60.

49

How shells grow

A shell is a mollusc's covering for its soft body and is a protection against its enemies. It is formed from a thin layer called a mantle, which covers the body of the mollusc. The mantle secretes a limy substance which hardens on contact with air or water to form a shell.

The shell is made up of three layers: the periostracum, the pigmented layer and calcium layer. The periostracum is a very thin layer which protects the shell and hides its natural colour. Shells found on the beach are usually colourful because the periostracum has been rubbed away while the shell was drifting in the sea. Some shells, like cowries, do not have a periostracum.

The calcium layer is fine and smooth, and is sometimes mother-of-pearl. The pigmented layer is the colourful part of the shell.

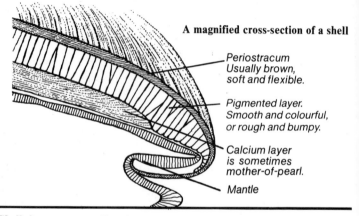

A magnified cross-section of a shell

Periostracum
Usually brown,
soft and flexible.

Pigmented layer.
Smooth and colourful,
or rough and bumpy.

Calcium layer
is sometimes
mother-of-pearl.

Mantle

Shell rings

When food supply is poor, shells grow thicker rather than larger forming these growth rings.

When food supply is good, mollusc grows fast, so shell grows quickly and thinly.

Shells in tropical seas are usually bigger, more colourful, thinner and lighter than shells of the same family that live in colder waters.

Molluscs grow faster when there is a plentiful food supply than when it is cold and there is little food. As a mollusc grows, so does its shell. Shells grow at a fairly steady rate if there is enough food.

On bivalves you can see a growth pattern that is similar to the annual growth rings seen in tree trunks.

Biology of a mollusc

A mollusc's body is soft and has no skeleton. The shell is the animal's protection into which it can withdraw when in danger. The body is usually divided into the head, which consists of a mouth and nerve centre, a muscular foot, and the visceral mass, which contains its organs, like the heart and digestive system. The body is completely surrounded by the mantle, from which the shell is formed.

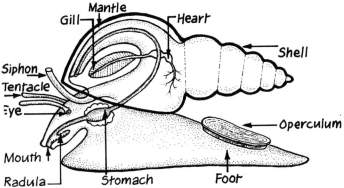

A **gastropod** has a coiled shell with an opening which relates to its body size. On its foot it often has an operculum which seals the shell opening when the animal is inside. On its head are two pairs of tentacles; one pair contains the sense organs, and the other usually has eyes at either the top or the bottom. It has a radula or "tongue", which is a horny strip with tiny teeth, used to scrape at either seaweed, or animals (dead or living). It lays live young or eggs that hatch into miniature snails or free-swimming larvae called "veligers" (see page 52).

A **bivalve** has two shells which are hinged together with little "teeth" which interlock. The shells are kept closed by a pair of strong muscles and opened by a rubbery ligament. The muscles are visible as scars on the inside of the shells. Some bivalves live attached to rocks and others burrow in sand, rock or mud. Bivalves breathe and feed by drawing water into the gills. The gills absorb oxygen and collect tiny particles of animal and vegetable matter that are passed into the mouth. Bivalves lay eggs that hatch into free-swimming veligers.

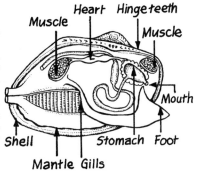

51

Life cycle of a mollusc

Some species can be found all over the world, while others live only in certain small areas of the world. One of the reasons for this is that some start life in their proper habitat and never move far from it, while others have a time of free-floating in the sea. These could be carried miles from where they were hatched, before they sink to the bottom, where they may or may not find a suitable habitat.

Some molluscs are laid as eggs and hatch into tiny shelled "crawlers," and some are born as "crawlers." Others are laid as eggs and hatch into "veligers." A veliger is free-swimming and has the beginning of a shell. It lives in the sea with the tiny animals and plants called plankton.

Thousands of the tiny veligers are hatched from hundreds of egg capsules. So many are laid because hundreds are eaten by fish and other animals, and others never find a suitable habitat. In fact only a few ever live to become adults.

The tiny shelled "crawlers" are born into their own habitat, so fewer need to be laid to make sure that some survive.

This shows the different stages in the life of a gastropod called a Murex.

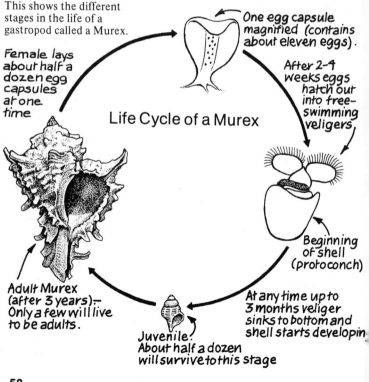

Life Cycle of a Murex

One egg capsule magnified (contains about eleven eggs).

After 2-4 weeks eggs hatch out into free-swimming veligers.

Beginning of shell (protoconch)

At any time up to 3 months veliger sinks to bottom and shell starts developin

Juvenile. About half a dozen will survive to this stage

Adult Murex (after 3 years)— Only a few will live to be adults.

Female lays about half a dozen egg capsules at one time

How a mollusc moves

Although molluscs do not have legs to walk on, they have a muscular foot. They move either to find a better food supply or to escape from their enemies.

Gastropods usually move by a rippling movement of the foot: some lighter species swim this way.

Some bivalves expand and contract their foot to move through mud and sand. Others clap their shells together and by shooting water out from between their shells, move forward or backward.

A gastropod

A Gastropod has three contraction waves that move from the back of the foot to the front.

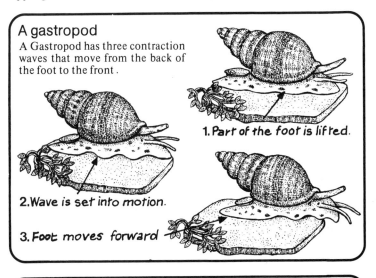

1. Part of the foot is lifted.

2. Wave is set into motion.

3. Foot moves forward

A bivalve

The file shell claps its two shells together to move forward.

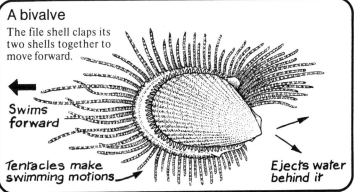

Swims forward

Tentacles make swimming motions

Ejects water behind it

Where shells live . . .

Molluscs have adapted to particular habitats which give them the best possible chance of survival, where they can find food, protection from their enemies, and where they can breed successfully. Here are some examples of different habitats and the type of shells you find in them.

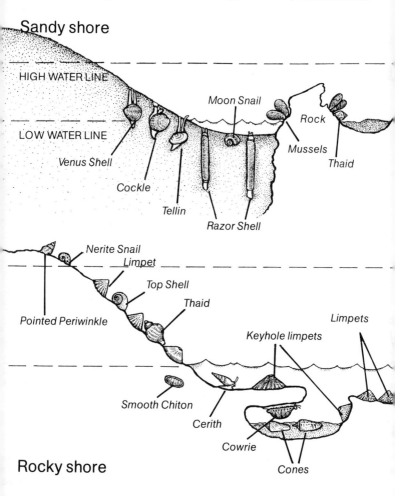

Sandy shore

HIGH WATER LINE

LOW WATER LINE

Moon Snail

Rock

Mussels

Thaid

Venus Shell

Cockle

Tellin

Razor Shell

Nerite Snail

Limpet

Top Shell

Thaid

Pointed Periwinkle

Limpets

Keyhole limpets

Smooth Chiton

Cerith

Cowrie

Cones

Rocky shore

...rocky and sandy shores

Shells which are not related often have similar shapes because they live in the same kinds of habitats. For instance, mud-living species (see next page) may have side spines or thin spires to steady themselves. Shells attached to rocks are usually smooth and broad; rocky-bottomed dwellers have heavy, bumpy shells. In coral (see next page), frilly spines can act as camouflage.

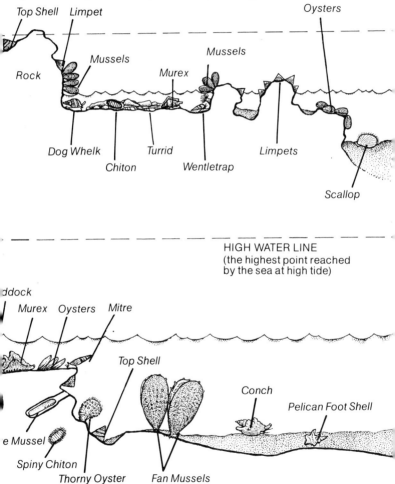

Top Shell Limpet

Rock

Mussels

Murex

Mussels

Oysters

Dog Whelk

Chiton

Turrid

Wentletrap

Limpets

Scallop

HIGH WATER LINE
(the highest point reached
by the sea at high tide)

ddock

Murex Oysters Mitre

Top Shell

Conch

Pelican Foot Shell

e Mussel

Spiny Chiton

Thorny Oyster

Fan Mussels

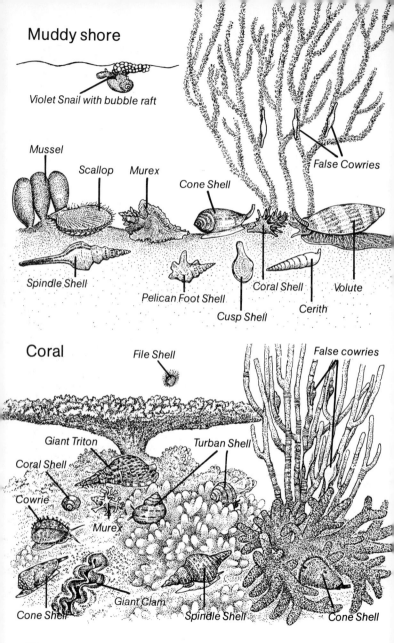

Muddy shore

Violet Snail with bubble raft

Mussel

Scallop

Murex

Cone Shell

False Cowries

Spindle Shell

Pelican Foot Shell

Cusp Shell

Coral Shell

Cerith

Volute

Coral

File Shell

False cowries

Giant Triton

Turban Shell

Coral Shell

Cowrie

Murex

Cone Shell

Giant Clam

Spindle Shell

Cone Shell

Collecting shells

What to take

You need a plastic bucket, bags or jam jars to put your shells in, and a sieve for the sand. Tie string around them so you can hang them around your neck and keep your hands free for turning rocks and picking up shells. It's a good idea to make notes about what you find, so take a notebook and pencil wrapped in a plastic bag.

Where to look

Shells can be found on most beaches but sometimes they are hard to see. On the previous pages you can find out what type of shells to expect on a particular shore.

A good time to start looking is at low tide. You can start at the level of high water, and look among the debris washed up there. Turn seaweed over as shells may still be clinging to it. Look for shells as you walk down to the sea and as the tide comes in, walk back and collect any shells that the sea washes up.

After a storm the beach is always worth searching. You should be able to find some quite large shells. Many will be damaged but by looking carefully you may find some good specimens.

On sandy beaches look out for microshells. These are tiny, but are no less interesting than the larger ones and can easily be missed. Sieve the sand and see what you find.

On rocky shores it is best to collect at low tide. Look in rock pools and tiny crevices. Turn small rocks over to see what is underneath, but remember to put them back where you found them.

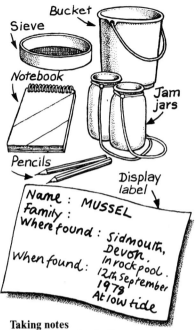

Bucket
Sieve
Notebook
Jam jars
Pencils
Display label

Name : MUSSEL
Family :
Where found : Sidmouth, Devon.
In rock pool.
When found : 12th September 1978
At low tide

Taking notes

When you find a shell, make a note of its name, where and when you found it. If you don't know the name, look it up when you get home. Without this information a shell is just a shell, but with it, the shell becomes a scientific specimen. When you get home you can put all this information on a display label or index card.

Before setting off down the beach to collect shells take note of the times of the tides to make sure that you don't get stranded.

Cleaning and storing shells

Cleaning shells

If a shell is covered in weed or barnacles, or still has its periostracum, (see page 50) you can clean it. Put it in an equal mixture of warm water and household bleach (wear rubber gloves when mixing.) Leave it overnight. In the morning brush the shell very carefully with a toothbrush. Don't polish or varnish shells. If they look dull and colourless, wipe them over with a cloth soaked in light oil or medicinal paraffin.

If you want to keep the periostracum, don't leave the shell in the bleach for longer than ten minutes.

Use the toothbrush very lightly, as the periostracum tends to flake off when dry.

Never put the operculum (see page 51) in bleach because it will dissolve.

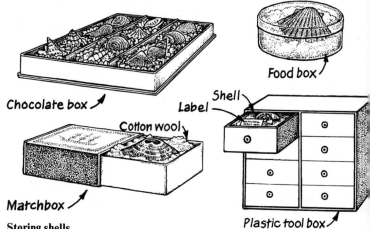

Chocolate box

Food box

Matchbox

Label

Shell

Cotton wool

Plastic tool box

Storing shells

Keep your collection in some sort of order. Try to keep the families together, and then store them either by locality or in date order. Put the scientific information on a card and store it with the shell.

Always store shells away from sunlight or they will fade, become dried out and fragile.

There are many different ways of storing shells. It is possible to buy multi-drawered cabinets for shells, but you can also put them separately in plastic bags and store them neatly in a drawer or use matchboxes, small tins, plastic food containers, chocolate boxes or plastic tool boxes.

Books to read

The Encyclopedia of Shells.
S. Peter Dance (Blandford)
*The Hamlyn Guide to Shells of
the World.* A.P.H. Oliver (Hamlyn)
Identification of British Mollusca.
Gordon Beedham (Hulton
Educational Publications)
Seashells. S. Peter Dance (Hamlyn)
*Seashells of the British and
European Coasts.* J. Arrecgros
(Spectrum Colour Books)
*A Field-guide to Shells of the
Atlantic and Gulf Coasts.*
Percy A. Morris (Peterson Field
Guide Series)
Shells of the World. A. P. H. Oliver
(Hamlyn)
What Shell is that? Neville Coleman
(Hamlyn)
A good Italian shell magazine,
in English, called *La Conchiglia* is
available from The Editor,
La Conchiglia, Via C Frederici 1,
00147 Rome, Italy.

Useful addresses

If you write to these shell clubs
they should be able to give you
information on shells in their areas.
The Secretary, *The British Shell
Collectors' Club,* c/o 125 Lonsdale
Drive, Rainham, Kent.
The Secretary, *Hawaiian
Malacological Society,* PO Box 10391,
Honolulu, Hawaii 96916, USA.
Australia has a number of local
shell clubs. The *Keppel Bay Shell
Club* produces a magazine called
Keppel Bay Tidings. Write to the
Secretary, PO Box 264, Yeppoon,
Queensland 4703, Australia.
For a directory of the many shell
clubs in America write to
Tom Rice, Sea and Shore
Publications, PO Box 33, Port
Gamble, Washington 98354, USA.

Tips on collecting

When your friends go on trips to
other parts of the country or to
other countries ask them to collect
shells for you. You can then see
how species vary from area to area.
You can also arrange to swap shells
with your friends when you have
been away.

When you are at the seaside
ask the fishermen to keep shells
that get tangled up in their nets
for you.

Do not take live specimens of
shells, however beautiful they
might look. Some species around
the world are now very rare
because so many have been
collected.

When you have collected shells
from the seaside and want to
know more about a particular
family, or about shells in general,
visit your local museum and ask
to see their shell collection; most
museums have one.

Many museums have space to
display only a part of their
collection. If there is a particular
shell family you want to see, ask
the museum staff. They will
probably be helpful if they
know that you are interested.

Glossary

Algae - water plants eg seaweed.

Aperture - opening in gastropod shell (see page 49).

Beak - earliest formed part of the bivalve shell (see page 49).

Bivalve - mollusc with two shells hinged together.

Body whorl - the last and largest coil of a gastropod shell.

Columella - central pillar at the opening of a gastropod shell (see page 49).

Crawlers - young molluscs that have a shell when they hatch from the egg.

Ear - small flat pieces on a bivalve on either side of the hinge (see page 49).

Gastropod - mollusc with a single shell which is usually coiled.

Habitat - a particular place where animals and plants live.

Hinge - the area where the two halves of bivalves join and where the ligament and teeth are situated.

Hinge teeth - interlocking device which keeps the two shells of the bivalve together (see pages 49 and 51).

Juvenile - a young mollusc.

Ligament - elastic material which opens the two shells of a bivalve when the muscles are relaxed.

Lip - outer edge of the opening of a gastropod shell.

Mantle - fold of "skin" which covers the mollusc's body (see pages 50 and 51).

Microshells - very small species of shells.

Muscle scars - marks on the inside of a bivalve where the muscles, which pull the shells together, were attached (see page 51).

Operculum - horny material on the gastropod foot that seals the shell opening when the animal is inside (see page 51).

Periostracum - a thin layer of horny material that protects the shell and usually hides its natural colour (see page 50).

Protoconch - the first formed whorl of a gastropod shell (see pages 49 and 52).

Sculpture - a raised pattern on a shell.

Radula - a horny "tongue" with tiny teeth, used for scraping at algae or animals (dead or alive).

Shoulder - an angular lump or ridge on the side of the body whorl.

Siphonal canal - a channel at the bottom of the gastropod shell opening (see page 49).

Species - shells that breed together and almost always look alike (see page 4).

Spines - spikes growing out from a shell.

Spire - part of the gastropod shell above the body whorl.

Suture - the place where two whorls join (see page 49).

Valve - one half of a bivalve shell.

Varix (plural: varices) - a thickened part of a shell, which was formed when there was a pause in the shell's growth.

Veliger - a free-swimming stage of a mollusc, before it becomes an adult (see page 52).

Whorl - one complete coil of a gastropod shell.

Checklist

When you find a shell, write the date when it was found on the checklist, and where you found it. You can also mark off other species that are not found in Britain or North America if you see them in museums or find them in shell shops.

	Date seen	Where found		Date seen	Where found
Ark Shells			File Shells		
Augers			Frog Shells		
Bittersweet Clams			Giant Clams		
Bubble Shells			Hairy Tritons		
Button Shells			Hammer/Tree Oysters		
Carditas			Harp Shells		
Carrier shells			Helmet Shells		
Cephalopods			Hoof Shells		
Chitons			Horn Shells		
Cockles			Jewel Boxes		
Cone Shells			Keyhole Limpets		
Coral Snails			Lucines		
Cowries			Limpets		
Crown Conches			Margin Shells		
Dog Cockles			Mitres		
Dog Whelks			Moon Snails		
Dove Shells			Murex Shells		
False Cowries			Mussels		
False Tritons			Nerite Snails		
Fan Mussels			Nut Shells		
Fig Shells					

	Date seen	Where found		Date seen	Where found
Nutmegs			Turban Shells		
Olives			Turrets		
Ormers/Abalones			Turrids		
Ostrich Foot Shells			Tusk Shells		
Pearl Oysters			Vase Shells		
Pelican Foot Shells			Venus Clams		
Periwinkles			Violet Shells		
Piddocks			Volutes		
Oysters			Wedge Shells		
Razor Shells			Wentletraps		
Rock Shells			Whelks		
Saddle Oysters			Worm Shells		
Scallops					
Slipper Limpets					
Strombs					
Sundials					
Sunset Shells					
Surf Clams					
Tellins					
Thorny Oysters					
Top Shells					
Trough Shells					
Tulip Shells					
Tun Shells					

Index

Abalones, 9
Angel Wings, 46
Ark Shells, 37; Hairy, 37;
    Ponderous, 37
Angel's Wings, 46

Baby Ear, 15
Babylon, Channeled, 22
Banded Creeper, 13
Bitter Sweets, 37
Bivalves, 37-46; 51
Bleeding Tooth, 12
Bonnet, Japanese, 23;
    Scotch, 23
Bubble Shells, 36;
    Pacific, 36; White
    Banded, 36
Bull Mouth, 23
Bullia, Moroccan, 22
Button Shells, 34;
    Radiant, 34

Callidan, 18
Canoe Shell, 35
Carditas, 38; European,
    38; Radiant, 38
Carrier Shells, 8;
    Mediterranean, 8;
    Pallid, 8
Cart Rut Shell, 20
Cephalopods, 49
Cerith, Common, 13
Chama, Leaf, 43
Chitons, 47; Lined, 47;
    Spiny, 47
Clams, Australian Surf,
    45; Giant, 39;
    Violet Surf, 45
Cockles, 39; Dog, 37;
    Egg, 39;
    Spiny Paper, 39
Cock's Comb, 41
Conches, 24; 25;
    Crown, 27; Fighting,
    24; Lister's, 24
Cone Shells, 28; Court,
    28; Fig, 28; Prince, 28
Coquina, Giant False,
    44; Panama, 44
Coral Snails, 21;
    Meyendorff's, 21;
    Violet, 21

Cowries, 34; Atlantic, 34;
    Egg, 35; Elongated
    Egg, 35; European, 34;
    False, 35; Humpback,
    34; Little Deer, 34;
    Pustulate, 35;
    Sieve, 34
Crown Conches, 27
Crucibles, 7
Cup and Saucer, 7
Cuttlefish, 48

Distaff Spindle, 16
Dog Cockles, 37
Dog Whelks, 22;
    Unicolour, 22;
    Wolff's 22
Dove Shells, 36;
    Rustic, 36
Drupe, Red Mouth, 20
Duck Foot Shells, 26
Dye Shells, 20

Ear Shells, 9; Ridged, 9
Eastern Lion's Paw, 42

False Cowries, 35
False Tritons, 21;
    Giant, 21
Fan Mussels, 46
Fig Shells, 15;
    Spotted, 15
File Shells, 42;
    Iredale's Giant, 42
Foot Shells, Duck, 26;
    Ostrich, 26;
    Pelican, 26;
    West African Bird, 26
Frog Shells, 17;
    Blood Stained, 17

Gastropods, 6-36; 51; 53
Giant Clams, 39; Fluted,
    39; Long, 39

Hairy Tritons, 17
Hallia, 33
Hammer/Tree Oysters, 40
Harp Shells, 28;
    Articulated, 28;
    Rose, 28;

Helmet Shells, 23,
    King, 23
Hoof Shells, 7
Horn Mouth, Leafy, 19
Horn Shells, 13
Horse's Hoof, 7
Hungarian Cap, 7

Jewel Boxes, 43

Keyhole Limpets, 6;
    Great Panama, 6;
    Italian, 6
Knorr's Worm, 14

Latirus, Knobbly, 16
Limpets, 6; Eye, 6;
    Italian, 6; Keyhole, 6;
    Mediterranean, 6;
    Slipper, 7;
    Tortoiseshell, 6
Little Fox, 29
Long Ancilla, 31
Lucines, 45; Buttercup,
    45; Orb, 45

Mantle, 50
Margin Shells, 30;
    Desjardin's, 30; Loup,
    30; Orange, 30;
    Philippine, 30; Pink,
    30; Striper, 30
Mitres, 29; Cone, 29;
    Dactylus, 29; Diadem,
    29; Thread, 29
Moon Snails, 15;
    Colourful Atlantic, 15;
    Lightning, 15
Murex Shells, 18; 19;
    Dye, 18; Pinnatus, 19;
    Ramose, 18;
    Stainforth's, 18;
    Zambo's, 19
Mussels, 38; Blue, 38;
    Date, 38; Fan, 46;
    Horse, 38; Yellow, 38

Nautilus, Brown Paper,
    48; Chambered, 48;
    Paper, 48
Necklace Shells, 15

Needle Tooth, 16
Needle Whelks, 13
Neptune, New
    England, 22
Nerite Snails, 12;
    Chameleon, 12
Nut Shells, 37;
Nutmegs, 17;
    Common, 17

Olives, 31; Fat, 31; Lady,
    31; Red Mouth, 31;
    Tent, 31
Operculum, 49; 51
Ormers, 9; Black, 9
Ostrich Foot Shells, 26
Oysters, 41; European,
    41; Flat, 40; Hammer,
    40; Pearl, 40; Saddle, 41;
    Thorny, 43; Tree, 40;
    White Hammer, 40

Pagoda, Mawa's, 21
Pearl Oysters, 40
Pelican Foot Shells, 26
Pelican's Tongue, 35
Pen Shells, 46
Periostracum, 50
Periwinkles, 12; Flat, 12;
    Southern, 12
Peruvian Hat, 7
Piddocks, 46
Purple Snail, Dwarf, 8

Radula, 51
Ramshorn, 48
Razor Shells, 46
Rock Shells, 20;
    Three Winged, 19;
    Wide Mouthed, 20
Roman Shield, 6

Saddle Oysters, 41
Sanguin, Stanger's, 45
Scallops, 42; Australian,
    42; Calico, 42;
    Pilgrim's, 42
Screw Shells, 12;
    European, 12
Shark Eye, 15
Simnia, False, 35

Slipper Limpets, 7
Snipe Head, 26
Star Shells, 9; Modest, 9
Strombs, 24; 25;
    Granular, 24; Sail, 25;
    Scorpion, 24;
    Spider, 24
Sundials, 8; Giant, 8
Sunrise Shell, 44
Sunset Shells, 45
Surf Clam, Australian,
    45; Violet, 45

Tellins, 44; Flat, 44
Thaid, Garland, 20
Thorny Oysters, 43;
    Red, 43
Tibia, Dwarf, 25;
    Martin's, 25; Powis',
    25; Spindle, 25
Tooth Shell, Elephant,
    47; Rosy, 47
Top Shells, 10; 11; Coral,
    11; Dolphin, 11; Kelp,
    10; Lined, 11;
    Pheasant, 11; Pyramid,
    10; Radiant, 10; Snake
    Skin, 10; Strawberry,
    10; Yellow Sponge, 10
Triton, Angular, 17;
    Atlantic, 17; Distorsio,
    17; False, 21; Hairy, 17
Trough Shells, 45
Tulip Shells, 16;
    Fischer's, 16;
    Hunter's, 16
Tun Shells, 14; Banded,
    14; Partridge, 14
Turban Shells, 9;
    Tapestry, 9
Turkey Wing, 37
Turrets, 12
Turrids, 14; Rose, 14
Tusk Shells, 48
Typhis, Cuming's, 19

Vase Shells, 26
Veliger, 51; 52
Venus Clams, 43;
    Keller's, 43; Lamellate,
    43; Tent, 43
Venus Comb, 18

Violet Shells, 8
Volutes, 32-33; Algarve,
    32; Beautiful, 33;
    Cuming's, 32;
    Ethiopian, 32;
    Damon's, 33; Hebrew,
    32; Imperial, 32;
    Junonia, 3; Neptune,
    33; Snowflake, 33

Wedge Shells, 44
Wentletraps, 13;
    Crenulated, 13;
    Precious, 13
Whelks, 23; Dog, 22;
    Fig, 27; Lightning, 27
Winkles, 12
Worm Shells, 14